STRAY

SUMMER

Once Over Series

By: Shonda Czeschin Fischer

Dedicated to my Great Grandmother Bessie, who taught me how wonderful strawberries taste. I have so many wonderful memories thanks to you.

For I know the plans I have for you, declares The Lord, plans to prosper you and not to harm you, plans to give you hope and a future. Jeremiah 29:11

Pubished in the United States of America
Cover Designer: April Clark
Editor: Fixer Fairy

Prologue

ONCE OVER, COLORADO
JULY 1873

The hot day brought about clear blue skies that foretold of a beautiful summer day, wiping her hand across the sweat beading on her forehead, she thought, what could be better than fishing with Collin today? The creek that rolled past the outcropping of smaller mountains on the north side of Triple B Ranch briskly flowed, the cold water turned into a heavenly respite from the heat of the day.

Viola rushed through her chores and dinner, fidgety with the excitement of the cool mountain stream and Collin.

After wrapping some cookies and a fresh jar of lemonade, Viola rushed along the base of the mountain to an open stream that was crystal clear, braids swinging as she went.

Viola's mind drifted to how Collin could talk to her about anything, his wit and how he laughed when she told him jokes. Collin's lean body, sun-kissed from long hours in the sun and dreamy chocolate eyes made her insides flutter. The best part of Collin McKenny was that he did not make her feel like she was a giggly little girl. He made her feel like she mattered, that she was pretty by the way he always called her beautiful when he saw her.

Collin may be a few years older than her, but he never treated her like a child. Humming a tune as she skipped toward their particular fishing hole, she felt all the butterflies fluttering in her stomach at spending time with Collin.

"Margie, you sure do smell pretty!" Viola stopped. Was that Collin's voice she heard? Why was he talking to Margie? She hated to fish and would not want to mess up her fancy dress. Margie was a prissy girl who did not like to get her hands dirty or climb trees. She wanted to walk around all gussied up and act like she was better than everyone else. She was not any fun at all. Why would Collin bring her along?

"Collin, it's my new lilac soap," Margie crooned. Viola could not believe her ears; as she crouched beside a boulder, she could see Collin and Margie. Margie in her Sunday best dress and parasol with Collin holding her hand. He looked as if he was going to kiss her!

Viola spun away and ran back to the ranch, cookies and lemonade were all forgotten except for the rumpled towel in her hand.

Chapter 1

The whoosh of the engine as it shuddered into the station woke Viola with a start. At the base of Viola's neck, a knotted mass started a throbbing in her head from sleeping in an awkward position. How had she slept so soundly on this monster of a contraption? She must look a mess!

Dusting off her dull brown dress to rid the soot she uncoiled her hair, twisting and repining made her feel a little tidier.

——The train ride had been long and dusty with seats that did not accommodate one's back side. Viola, glad to be done with finishing school, needed a break from the city. Spending the summer with Grandmother in Once Over was just what she needed. The thought of those luscious ruby red strawberries made her stomach grumble; it had been a hours since lunch.

"Once Over," a conductor bellowed.

"Once Over, what kind of name is that?" an irritating voice grated across the expanse of the car.

Viola turned to a rather ostentatious purple feathered hat, flouncing side to side on a lady's head, her mouth pulled into a pucker as if she ate a lemon.

Summoning a right attitude to answer politely, Viola coughed into her handkerchief, gaining the lady's attention.

"If I may explain, the town founder named it that. When the wagon trains came through, this was the last mountain to pass over, and things got a might more comfortable after that. The problem was that getting over was extremely dangerous, many didn't survive, so they decided to stay right here and form Once Over because once over, the wagon train had a much more manageable trip." she proudly announced.

With a shameless look, the boisterous lady harumphed and folded her hands on her lap. She was muttering that it still was a rather unusual name for a town.

Viola smoothed her skirt's front; she picked up her reticule and made her way out onto the busy platform. *Some people should keep their opinions to themselves.*

Looking around for her grandmother's foreman, as people rushed by, she spotted a handsome enough man looking above heads as the noisy crowds hurried to get to their destinations. Earthy brown eyes landed on her and wandered from the pert little hat on her head to the pointy kid boots on her feet.

Straightening her shoulders, she waved her arm, signaling Mr. Emerson.

"Miss Branson? You sure have grown into a beautiful young lady, you look just like Bessie when she was younger." Grabbing Viola's trunk, Jude lifted it into the wagon while extending a hand to help Viola onto the seat.

Looking into his weathered face with a tired smile, Viola curiously asked, "How is grandma doing?"

"As ornery as ever, just like always! Getting her to slow down is like pulling teeth from a mountain lion."

"That doesn't surprise me," Viola smiled.

Jude and Viola talked about the ranch between patches of silence as they rode along the rut-filled road. The grand mountain jutted up out of the vast green and lavender patched land. Nestled among the cozy pines stood a two-story log home with its cozy front porch, expansive barns, and Grandmother's ruby red strawberry garden, in all its glory. The Triple B Ranch and its many pastures of steer stood out like a cowboy's dream.

A feeling of warmth and love spread through the pit of Viola's stomach; why had she not been back to visit in the last five years? She had missed her grandmother, the jam-making sessions, not to mention the best food on this side of civilization.

Collin McKinney, that was why. Just thinking of that cowboy made her blood boil! Collin and Viola had spent every summer together as children, even liked each other at one time, until that hot July day. Viola could still remember that day as if it were yesterday. The fresh smell of pine and cattle drifted on the breeze as Jude brought the clamoring wagon to a stop.

The front door of the sturdy two-story house was flung open.

"There's my beautiful, long-lost granddaughter!" Stepping out of the house in a faded dress and a clean apron tied around her front,

Grandmother clapped her hands together and threw her arms open wide.

Eyes filling with emotion, Viola took in her grandmother's small frame as Jude helped her from the wagon.

Grandmother pulled Viola into a warm hug. She melted into the warm embrace that smelled of vanilla and cinnamon just as she remembered.

Drinking in the familiar sight of the white-capped mountain, pastures of green grass dotted with tiny purple flowers feeding the cattle grazing about, she followed Grandmother into the house as Jude took her trunks to her room.

"Let me get a look at you, girl; you sure have grown up, look as pretty as a daisy too. I will get you a cup of tea and warm up some of my stew. I know you had a long tiring trip; I will have Jude bring the washtub in for a nice long soak."

Viola smiled a weary smile, "That sounds wonderful."

Hefting up the tub to his shoulder, Jude hauled the washtub to her room.

Perched on a handsomely made washstand were a towel and sweet-smelling soap.

Grandmother commenced filling the tub with hot water as she hummed a tune.

She patted Viola's shoulder, "Why don't you have a soak while I make your tea and warm- up that stew. We can sit a spell before you retire for the night."

"Thank you, Grandmother, I have had a long day. That sounds wonderful."

Viola woke with a satisfying stretch and a slow, lazy smile on her lips at the smell of coffee. She felt refreshed. What a beautiful morning, a great day for adventure, or at least a thought of one. First, she needed to do whatever she could to make life easier for her grandmother.

"Viola girl, how did you sleep"?

"Like a baby."

"Well, child, sit, let me pour you a cup of coffee and dish up your breakfast. Once breakfast is out of the way, we can start picking berries, and I will need more jars and wax for sealing. We can take the wagon into town, stop at the mercantile, and while the jars are loaded, how about we stop at Rosebud's and have some lunch? Catch up some; grandmother caroled," as she squeezed Viola's hand.

The day was perfect, with a soft breeze of mountain air drifting in to keep a nip of cool in the air. With dishes washed and put away, Viola and grandmother started for town. Grandmother perched on the seat beside Viola taking the reins in her hands gave it a firm slap against the horse's rumps. The rattle of the wagon with its sway relaxed Viola to the point of drowsiness. The comfortable silence between them was like a blanket the made you feel safe and warm if you needed it.

Grandmother pointed out flowers growing wild along the road as they talked about how exciting spring was in these parts.

Chapter 2

Collin strode through the livery, happy to finally be getting the dainty palomino sold. A great little filly for a proper city lady to ride.

Counting his money, Collin thought about his grumbling stomach that was ready for a meal. Might as well head to Rosebud's for some of Rosie's meat pies, then to the bank. Collin was steadily making progress to buying a small herd that could make him a comfortable living. Four years ago, today would mark the day he decided to stop living by the seat of his britches and make something of himself.

With Pa and Ma, both gone now, all he had was his sister Darla. Darla had married and moved to Texas; Collin was now by himself looking after the homestead. Life had been rough and left a bitter taste in his mouth; he was ready for more.

In front of Rosebud cafe, stepping up on the boardwalk, was a jaw-dropping beauty with blonde curls attached to a perfect curvy creature who was chatting with Bessie Branson. Collin stumbled as if in a daze; she looked familiar, and Collin was adamant about finding out who she was.

"Mrs. Branson, Ma'am," Collin tipped his cowboy hat as he approached the women. "Mighty fine day to grab a bite of Rosie's meat pies."

"Mr. McKinney, how are you this fine day? You remember my lovely granddaughter, Viola?"

Tongue-tied Collin smiled and just stared; Viola had turned into a stunning woman!

"Mr. McKinney," Viola heard herself huff. "Grandmother, we need to be going if we are going to accomplish everything we have to do today."

"Yes, of course, Viola. Mr. McKinney, would you like to join us for lunch?"

Collin caught a faint grimace on Viola's face; why did she not look happy to see him? I do not think she is pleased about the invite, well, we will see about that.

"It would be my pleasure, Mrs. Branson. Ladies, after you," Collin held the door open for the ladies as they made their way into the busy establishment. A smirk pulled at his lips as Viola nodded her thanks.

Windows lined the front of the establishment as tables formed neat rows to accommodate four guests each. The aroma of food filled the air making Collin's mouth water.

Collin grinned, pulling the chair out; he seated Viola then turned to seat Grandmother.

The waitress came to take orders, pouring them each a glass of water. "What can I get everyone." Emma perched her hand on her hip. "Viola Branson, is that you? It has been a while since I have seen you."

"It has been a while; I'm glad to be back helping my grandmother with her famous strawberry jam, just like when I was little," Viola smiled.

An eager smile formed on Emma's lips; "Let's get together sometime, maybe have tea."

"That sounds wonderful," Viola said, giving Emma an excited smile.

"What can I get everyone? Emma's eyes danced as she turned to Collin.

Collin winked at her, "I'll take the meat pie."

Emma's face turned bright red, "Sure thing, Mr. McKenny."

"What can I get you, ladies?" Emma asked.

"What's the special today," Grandmother smiled sweetly.

Emma rattled off the special, which included mashed potatoes, roast beef with brown gravy, green beans, and fluffy rolls.

"I will take the special," Grandmother answered.

Viola looked up and said, "I'll take the same, thank you."

Emma walked off with the orders, smiling at Collin as she went.

Collin looked up at Viola; he could tell he hit a sore spot. He could not help but smirk at the look she was giving him.

Emma returned with their food, interrupting the sudden tension in the air.

Collin could not resist; he smiled an all-tooth smile at Emma. With a tip of his hat, he warmly thanked Emma for bringing their food.

Viola rolled her eyes at the flirtatious display.

Lunch consisted of small talk of the weather, the price of cattle, and of course, Viola's trip to Colorado.

"Ladies, lunch is on me today. It's not every day I get to spend time in such pleasant company." Collin said charmingly.

Politely thanking Mr. McKinney, Viola and Grandmother stepped out onto the boardwalk.

Grandmother turned to Collin, "Why don't you come by for dinner on Sunday? I plan to start making my strawberry jam; some of it should be ready by then. I'll send you home with a few jars."

Collin looked at Viola to see nothing but irritation on her pretty upturned face.

"Well, thank you, Mrs. Branson, that sounds mighty good. I think I'll take you up on that."

Viola took her grandmother's hand, and, with a pinched smile, she stated, "We need to be on our way if we intend to get some of that canning done by Sunday."

After saying their goodbyes, Grandmother and Viola strolled down the worn boardwalk to the mercantile. The clomping of horse's hooves and friendly greetings filled the atmosphere. Viola's head was full of thoughts of Collin, his tall, muscular frame with a chiseled chin, and the slightly worn look from not shaving that morning. His brown curls peeked out from under his worn cowboy hat. It took all her willpower not to reach out and finger those curls. She needed to shake those thoughts from her head. She should not be attracted to him; he broke her heart once before; she would not let it happen again.

What a flirt that Collin is; he has not changed at all. Oh, he makes me so mad! Viola's face puckered in thought. Viola was contemplating a headache on Sunday to get out of dinner with Collin when Grandmother cleared her throat.

"Viola dear, what has gotten into you? You were not the best with your manners today. Why you practically snubbed Mr. McKenny."

"Grandmother, that man is a flirtatious, cocky nuisance!"

"Viola, what would make you say a thing like that?"

With a stomp of her foot, she exclaimed, "He just rubs me the wrong way."

"He is to be our guest on Sunday; I want you to show your manners and be nice to him. Have I made myself clear on that?" Grandmother asked calmly.

"Yes, Grandmother," Viola softly commented.

Without any more discussion, they made their way into the mercantile. Viola looked at the rows of displayed wares, bolts of fabric stacked according to color, canned goods with labels facing outlined shelves. The store smelled of tobacco and spices. She inhaled the scent that brought back memories of her childhood before her parents had died. Today was not a day to think about those memories; she would see today as a blessing instead. Viola rubbed a creamy material with ~~little~~ tiny blues flowers through her fingers; she would love to buy some fabric to create a new dress. Maybe that would make dinner bearable on Sunday.

Crates of jars loaded in the wagon, along with canning wax and a bolt of cream fabric with tiny blue flowers that would make a lovely dress.

Mr. Tyree wrote down how much Bessie owed and showed her the figure. Grandmother lightly slapped the counter, put it on my tab; I'll be in to pay it next week.

Mr. Tyree looked up at Viola; "You must be little Viola? The last time you were here, you had braids and were only so tall." he motioned with his hand to his chest.

Viola laughed as she pulled out two sticks of hard butterscotch candy, one for her and one for her grandmother. Handing Mr. Tyree a coin, he put up his hand in protest, "On the house," he said, smiling.

Viola thanked him with her big smile and a wave as they left the store.

This town was what she had embedded in her heart. The longing for familiarity and family clung to her like smoke from a fire. The big city was noisy with people rushing about; no one cared about others, only where they were going and themselves. Viola had no desire to go back to St Joseph, Missouri. She had dreams of getting married, having children, and raising them here in Once Over.

Grandmother put her arm around Viola's shoulders and pulled her close. "I'm so happy your home granddaughter," she sighed.

Viola lay her head up against grandmother's shoulder. "Me too, Grandmother, me too."

Chapter 3

Farm life was good for Viola; she woke before the sun fully rose. The house's silence except for her feet that padded against the floor brought comfort and peace. She hurried through her morning ablutions, bursting with excitement for canning strawberries today. It was hot, hard work, made better by sampling the sticky, sweet goodness as they worked.

Stepping into the bright kitchen with its fancy cookstove and vast cabinets, Viola found Grandmother feeding wood into the stove.

"My, aren't you up early this morning." Grandmother pitched another log on to the fire.

"I'm excited to get this day started," Viola cheerfully exclaimed, tying the apron around her middle.

Jude walked into the cheery atmosphere, pouring himself a cup of coffee.

Grandmother began mixing the batter and pouring it into the cast iron pan. The golden fluffy cakes looked and smelled so delicious.

"Child, why don't you grab a few of those berries from the crates outside the door. Let's make a syrup to pour over these here hotcakes." Grandmother flipped another cake.

The berries mixed in sugar and vinegar boiled on the stove as Viola gently stirred the mixture. The heavenly smell rising from the pot making her mouth water.

Once the strawberries cooled some, Viola poured them in a fancy pitcher that she then sat on the table. Grandmother placed the hotcakes on the table with a fresh dish of creamy butter. Everyone sat down, bowing heads and holding hands as Grandmother said a prayer over their bountiful breakfast.

Lifting a bite of hotcake with strawberries to her mouth Viola let the warm flavors mingle on her tongue before swallowing the tasty morsel.

"Mm, this is what I have been anticipating since I have been back."

Grandma laughed a hardy laugh as she watched Viola's face. Yep, it was good to have her granddaughter back.

Viola began clearing off the table as Jude brought crates of berries in to be washed and hulled. Bags of sugar and jugs of vinegar set off to the side with jars, paper, and wax. It was going to be a long day.

The kitchen heated up fast with pots boiling away with the ripe strawberries. Viola poured the mixture into jars, setting them off the side to cool some.

Stretching, she splayed her hand on her lower back; using her other hand, she wiped the palm of it across her forehead. She had forgotten what back-breaking, hot work strawberry canning was. Viola glanced at Grandmother; she was still cleaning and cooking the strawberries as if it were child's play.

Grandmother caught Viola's eye and asked if she would like to take a small break.

Pouring the last precious drop, she let out a drained sigh.

Grandma poured Viola and herself a glass of sweet lemonade. Taking the lemonade, she followed Grandmother out to the front porch letting the door bang as she went. Viola sat in one of the sturdy rocking chairs that graced the front porch. Glancing out to the valley at the mountains she could hear the water rumbling over the rocks into the creek. Lifting the cool glass to her lips, guzzling the drink as sweat ran down the back of her dress, Violashe let herself get lost in the beauty. The smell of honeysuckle tickled her nose, closing her eyes she let peace engulf her. Too soon her thoughts turned to Sunday and Collin.

Viola wondered how she would ever get to sewing her new skirt as tired as she was. Collin was coming for dinner on Sunday; she wanted to look her best. She would show that no good flirt, Viola would be friendly, not give him the attention he thought all women should.

"Granddaughter, I think a day of swimming down at the creek would work some of these sore muscles out. We'll head down there once we finish these last few batches up; what do you say?"

"Oh, Grandmother! Viola gasped; "what an excellent idea. We have not done that since I was a little girl."

Grandmother lifted her face to the breeze, "I can make some sandwiches that we can take with us, just like old times."

Energized by the short break, Viola stood, stretching her sore back; taking Grandmother's glass, she headed back into the overly warm house to finish the job.

The birds chirping mingled into the cool breeze relaxing Viola as she and grandmother sat on an old quilt while they munched on sandwiches and sipped their sweet lemonade.

Laughter and voices carried on the breeze as they talked about sewing, strawberry jam making, and Viola's lackluster life back in Missouri.

A comfortable silence took over, looking out over the mountains and land that stretched before them brought joy and peace.

Viola let thoughts of staying here with grandmother for good swirl through her mind and take root. The beauty of the land and God's presence were all around them. Picking a slim green blade of grass and twirling it between her fingers, she would give it considerable thought. Viola's heart filled with emotion as she asked grandmother what she was thinking.

"Oh, taking in the beautiful day the Lord gave us and thinking about frying up a fat old chicken for dinner tomorrow night. I know how you love my fried chicken. I might even make us a strawberry pie for dessert."

Viola licked her lips, thinking about what grandmother was going to make. She had not had time to sew her skirt; maybe she could fix her hair differently, a little fancier than usual. Heck, she could even make that pie and show Collin just what he was missing.

Chapter 4

Collin chased the steer down and rounded him back to the pen. He had already sold a few heads; he was adding on to his herd nicely. He was not rich by any means; it paid the bills and then some.

His mind wandered back to Viola; she sure is a pretty thing. Those rosebud lips pouting as he accepted the invitation to Sunday dinner about did him in.

He had to get her out of his head; there was plenty to be done. The mortgage would be due on the farm shortly. He had to move this next heard off to market so he could pay it. Always something to fix or bills to pay, if he could only get ahead.

Hanging his head forward in deep thought, I need to hire someone. Scratching his chin, Collin decided to head to town tomorrow. He could ask Billy Mantle to help; the school had already been out a week; I am sure he would like to make a little extra money. He would be a good help, his Ma and Pa had five strapping sons that worked on and around the farm; those boys knew hard work.

The next morning following day dawn broke with sunlight streaming through the open window. Collin woke with a lazy yawn. Stumbling into the kitchen, he made himself a cup of strong coffee, got dressed, and started for the barn. There is no sense in wasting the day. Saddling his horse, Maverick, Collin figured he might as well get him a haircut while he was in town. His thoughts drifted back to lunch with Viola; she was so arrogant yet completely alluring. Her facial expressions said he annoyed her, but her eyes begged him to kiss her.

The woman was throwing out more mixed signals than a filly in a herd of stallions. What did he ever do to make her mad? The two of them use to be inseparable when they were younger. The two went fishing, riding horses, and even swimming when summer days got too hot. Now that they were adults, could they start that old friendship back up?

Collin rode in a slow cantor, his mind filled with one thing, Viola.

Green grass shooting up from the damp earth gave way to a much-traveled trail. The Mantle farm came into view, with so many questions floating around in his mind he did not hear the commotion coming from right in front of him; riding into the yard, he saw Billy trying to get a goat back into its pen.

Collin sat forward in the saddle, watching as the goat taunted Billy. The goat bleated, ran through the colorful flower garden, turned and ran back through it, trampling the flowers. Billy huffed and pleaded with the goat to get out. Finally, having enough, Billy turned as if to walk off, ignoring the old goat. The goat bleated several more times; Billy stopped and rested his hands on his knees; he was getting plumb tuckered out. The old goat let out one long bleat, running powerfully at Billy with head down, butting him right in the seat of his britches. Billy flew forward, sprawled out flat like a trampled flower.

Collin threw his head back and howled with laughter. That goat sure had an attitude; he was not one to be told what to do.

Billy sat up as if seeing stars and flung his cowboy hat on the ground.

"You stupid old goat, I ought a let Ma just fricassee your hide!" Billy stood, wiping the dirt off the front of his pants.

He strode to Collin, who was still snickering at the funny picture of Billy and his opinionated goat.

"Mr. McKenny, what are you doing out this way?"

Collin leaned back in the saddle, trying to compose himself.

"I wanted to see if you are interested in making a little extra money this summer."

Scratching behind his head, he squinted up at Collin, "Whatcha got in mind?"

"How about helping me with the herd? I need to rotate them to different pastures, get some breeding done then off to market."

Billy lifted his arm to wipe sweat from his brow, "I reckon that will be fine. Pa does not need any extra help right now, and I could use the money."

The two shook hands; Collin told Billy to be there at first light.

Billy would be a big help; maybe he would even get this herd to market on time.

Collin made his way to town with a merry jingle on his lips, feeling lighter than when he started this morning.

People milled about their morning chores with friendly greetings as Collin tied Maverick to the post in front of Floyd's barbershop. Noise from the train pulling into the station penetrated the air as the smell of bread and pastries lingered about the boardwalk.

His long waves fell into his eyes. as he pulled off his hat. Swiping his hand through the locks, he drew them back with one hand, placing the cowboy hat back onto his head as he headed into the establishment. Collin pushed open the door with a firm grip; a bell rang overhead.

"Well, look at the scoundrel of a tumbleweed that walked in my door." Floyd grinned with his two upper front teeth missing. "Bout time you get a haircut; looks like you been living out on the trail." Floyd slapped his hand on his pant leg, chuckling.

Slipping into the chair, Collin yanked his hat off and threw it onto a hat hook hanging on the wall.

"Starting to get a might warm, figured now was as good as time as any."

Floyd snipped away while engaging the conversation of cattle rustlers up north. Floyd shaved and was applying a nice warm damp towel over Collins's face when he asked if he had seen the Branson girl about town. Not caring about Collins's answer, Floyd went right on talking about how she was all grown up and easy on the eyes. "If I were only a few years younger," he whistled.

Collin thought he would flip right out of his chair at that statement. Chuckling to himself, he thanked Floyd for the cut and shave; flipping Floyd a coin while placing his hat on his head, he told Floyd to keep the change.

Opening the old door that stuck far too often, Collin strode onto the boardwalk, bumping into someone. A high-pitched squeal and boxes dropping pulled his attention around to a form bent over, picking up packages with a feathered silk hat askew on her head.

Leaning down, Collin started picking up boxes when a hand shot forward touching, his own. There stooped over the packages was none other than Margie Vancleet. Black ringlets hung down her back as she looked up at the intrusive being that ran her down.

Collin yanked his hand back as if being stung by a wasp. "M...Margie," he stuttered, "I didn't know you were back in Once Over."

Standing, Collin offered his hand out of good manners, helping Margie stand.

Batting eyelashes at him, Margie situated her fancy hat on her head. Cocking her head to the side, a smile took possession of her lips. "Well, Mr. McKenny, I came home for the summer to visit Momma and Daddy, maybe have a little fun in between," she replied with a flirty smile.

Lilac permeated the air as Collin stepped back. Bile burned the back of his throat as he stretched the collar around his neck. Now was a good time to turn tail and scram.

Pouty lips pressed together with an unwavering stance; Margie stepped forward in a determined pose.

Alarm bells going off in his head Collin turned just in time to see puckered lips as he made a hasty exit.

Swirling dust that stung the eyes chased after people and horses as they hurriedly went about their business as Collin joined them.

Untying Maverick, Collin climbed in the saddle posthaste, escaping from his past mistake.

With teeth still clenched, Collin wiped the sweat and dust from his face with a bandanna. That woman was barking up the wrong tree if she thought he would retake any interest in her.

Chapter 5

Sunday morning, the sun rose bright and early. Viola wanted to get a start on the day. Walking to the barn, the smell of cow, pungent with manure, woke a yearning for farm life in her; as she stood on tiptoes to retrieve the eggs, she hummed a hymn. Dragging a stool over to milk Anne, she laid her head on the big brown animal's flank; her mind drifted too how happy she was at being here.

Hurrying to the still quiet house with milk sloshing in the pail, Viola covered the bucket with a cloth. In no time at all, she had the stove going with water boiling in the coffee pot when grandma shuffled into the kitchen.

"My, you're up early with the chickens this morning!" exclaimed grandmother.

"Sit down and let me pour you a cup of coffee, grandmother. Thought I'd make us a quick bite of breakfast before we head to church."

"You're going to spoil these old bones; you keep this up."

Viola poured each of them a cup as she started cracking eggs into a pan.

"Where is Jude this morning?" Viola stretched to look out the kitchen window.

"He eats breakfast with the work hands, then they go to a cowboy service," grandmother waved her hand as if shooing a fly.

'The cowboys take turns hosting at some of the other farms; they have an outdoor service when the weather gets nice."

Viola flipped the eggs, eyes sparkling, as she thought of worshipping the King under the blue skies and majestic mountains.

Maybe she could talk Grandmother into going to a Cowboy service next Sunday; right now, she needed to hurry if she were going to look her best for the church in town.

Fingers trembled, pulling and tugging the gold locks into a tidy pile on top of Viola's head. Pins poking and prodding into place as a few wisps of hair softly fell around her face.

The soft flowing cream dress with dark blue flowers settled over her head and shoulders; Viola admired herself in the mirror. Feeling confident, she bounded down the steps picking up her bible from the kitchen table, patiently waiting on grandmother to gather her belongings as they made their way out to the buggy.

Children darted about as grownups visited in front of the handsome white clapboard church as the buggy pulled up beside the others tramping down the grass with it.

Climbing down briskly from the wagon, skirts swishing with a hand pressed firmly against her middle, Viola helped grandmother from the wagon, leading her through a slender double door as the church bells pealed into their incessant ringing.

Seating themselves into their familiar pew, a whiff of lavender mingled about tickling her nose as light a feather. Viola gazed about to see who the scent belonged to when a voice like nails on a chalkboard sounded in her ear.

"Well, you sure look…different." Viola swiveled about as she stood eye to eye with none other than Margie Vancleet.

"Margie, how are you?" Viola's conservative voice asked.

The conversation cut short as the Pastor asked everyone to begin singing the hymn *Shall We Gather at the River*. A powerful note rose from the organ as emotion-filled voices sprang into the air like a sweet offering. Service was endearing; Pastor preached on faith and love, filling the room with God's presence as it hovered over the congregation.

Viola felt a calmness envelop her; she would trust in God to lead her in her decision to stay in Once Over.

Families mingling with neighbors while shaking hands as the noise drifted out the door of the little church. Everyone was in a hurry to get outdoors into the bright sunlight.

Skirts rustling and lavender scent carried on the breeze as Margie caught up to Viola tucking her arm through hers.

"I declare, I didn't expect to see you in Once Over after being away so long. Miss me?" Margie chuckled.

Momentarily closing her eyes, Viola took a deep breath and sighed, "Something like that, it's been a while since I've seen my grandmother."

The air crackled with the tension that was a constant between the two; Margie smirked as she caught sight of Collin talking with the men by the buggies. Casting her gaze to follow Margie's, Viola saw Collin standing confidently with hands-on-hips laughing at something one of the men said.

Margie strolled to where Collin now stood, slipping her arm around his without so much as a glance back. Looking down at her with a startled look Collin said something Viola could not make out.

The air was being sucked out of her lungs as she coughed to regain her composure. Why did she even care?

Collin was a flirt just as much as Margie; they could have each other. Viola flounced ~~Flouncing~~ off with a stomp of her small kid boots, the sun beating down on her with an impressing weight as she dodged around children playing.

Viola looked around for grandmother just as hands gently closed around her waist and lifted her into the buggy. Letting out a squeal, Viola whipped her head around to see who was violating her in such a manner.

"What do you think you're doing," she blustered. With a heaving chest, hands firmly pressed to her throat, Viola gave Collin a look of disdain.

"I was trying to be a gentleman and help you into the wagon," he barked.

Fidgeting with her sleeves, Viola squeaked, "Don't you think you should have asked first? Did you help Margie up into her wagon as well?"

Now, why did she go and say that, and out loud none~~ the~~ theless?

"Why would I help Margie in her wagon?" Hands firmly planted on his hips, Collin gave Viola a perplexed look.

"Well, from what I saw earlier, I thought you were courting her."

"That woman, she has no claim on me! I have been patient with her, but I guess I will have to be firmer with her. I avoid her, but she is like a tick on a hound; she keeps sticking to me."

Viola smirked as she huffed under her breath, "Maybe you shouldn't have kissed her."

Heels clicking on the hard earth, Grandmother greeted Collin with a spring in her step and a smile on her face. "Be expecting you for supper, young man," she gave him her hand as he helped her into the wagon.

"Yes, ma'am, I will be there." With a tip of his hat, Collin sauntered off whistling.

Frying chicken permeated the air combined with yeast's fragrant aroma from the bread rising on the counter. Grandmother made the best-fried chicken with its golden-crusted skin that would rival anyone around.

Viola sliced strawberries, placing them in a bowl with sugar. The crust had been made and rolled out, just waiting for her to fill it. Once the pie was in the oven, she would need to get the potatoes peeled and ready for boiling. Humming a song as she went, her mind drifted to what it would be like to have a family of her own. She wanted children and could see herself with a handsome husband who she would work beside. Her mind was instantly going to Collin.

Her thoughts were interrupted as her grandmother snapped the towel to her backside and shooed Viola upstairs to clean up before Collin would arrive.

Her heart pounding only increased the anxious feeling that made her sour stomach turn over. Hurrying to change her dress and fix her hair, Viola could hear a knock at the front door.

Breathing a deep breath, she admired herself in the mirror; why was she feeling this way? Collin was a flirt with every female around; she had no interest in him at all. Now to make her heart listen to reason was another thing. A deep sigh filled the air around her; better greet their guest.

His hair neatly trimmed, wearing a dark blue shirt, setting off his chocolate eyes, and a freshly shaved face trained on Viola. She was in over her head, and he was so handsome!

"Mr. McKenny, hope you came with an appetite," Viola uttered as she started placing plates on the table.

"I think we know each other enough that you can call me Collin, don't you? To answer your question, yes, I'm starving." His stomach growled, causing Viola to smile.

Grandmother started placing bowls of steaming food on the table as Collin pulled the chair out for Viola; a hint of sandalwood mingled with leather engulfed her senses as she tried to focus on the food before her.

Once everyone was seated, her grandmother asked Collin to say grace.

"Dear heavenly Father, thank you for the bounty in front of us and the hands that prepared it. We thank you for the nourishment it will provide us and bless our fellowship as we enjoy each other's company on your day Lord," Amen, they chorused together.

Dishes clanked around the table as bowls of aroma drifted through the air.

Collin snuck a peek at Viola as she filled her plate. He swallowed the lump that formed in his throat as grandmother spoke up with a candid voice.

"What are you doing with that farm of yours? It seems it would be mighty hard to run by yourself. I reckon the days are tiresome for you," she stated, as Collin wiped his mouth with the cloth napkin that laid across his lap.

"It has been challenging. I ended up hiring Billy Mantle for the summer. With his help, the two of us should manage fine. Once I get my herd to market, I can use the money to expand, hire me a full-time ranch hand," His excitement evident in his voice. Collin then finished woofing down the remaining food on his plate without another word.

Viola's hands trembled as she picked up the platter of fried chicken, "Please help yourself too more. There is plenty. I do have a strawberry pie that I made this afternoon if you have room," she sputtered.

They locked eyes as if they were the only ones in the room. Viola's heart pounded so rapidly she was afraid everyone in the room could hear it.

A warm, lazy smile made its way across Collin's freshly shaved face as he cleared his throat," I believe I will take that pie instead, thank you."

Viola excused herself to cut the pie and serve it with a cup of coffee as Grandmother and Collin made small talk.

Cutting into the flaky, juicy, berry pie Viola's eyes took on a dreamy look as her mind thought on serving the sweet mannered cowboy. Thoughts of his flirtatious manner had her hating her traitorous heart.

Skirt rustling across the smooth wood floor with her emotions in check, she set pie and coffee in front of Collin before serving grandmother and herself.

"Mm, that was the most delicious pie I've ever eaten," Collin's expressive smile said he spoke the truth as he gently patted his stomach, "I need to walk off some of this food."

Grandmother's face broke into a broad smile, "Why don't you two go for a walk while I clean up. It sure is a beautiful evening."

Chapter 6

Beautiful hues clung to the sky as the sun was setting over the tops of the majestic mountains. Maverick whinnied as a tribute to the Western sky. The sounds of crickets and spring peepers adding their serenade as not to be left out.

Viola threw her wrap over her shoulder as the evening air had cooled considerably. Words would not come to her with the closeness of Collin and his masculine smell that rose around them as they started walking. Collin cleared his throat, looking out at the rich color of fields and cattle as they dotted the horizon.

A confident smile spread across his face as his baritone voice subduedly announced, "It sure is a beautiful evening." Viola hesitated, "Yes, it is."

Taking a deep breath, as if to say something, she peeked up at him through her long lashes to see Collin staring at her. She felt a jolt of emotion course through her. Viola had to remind herself he was a flirt and could not be trusted; he would never settle down.

"Viola, is there something I've done to make you not like me? You seem distant, like you do not want me around, even smirk at me like I am annoying. Pardon me for being so blunt."

Viola caught her bottom lip beneath her teeth; maybe she should tell him and get it out in the open. Viola huffed; her lips sewn in a grimace. "I saw you with Margie," there she had said it.

"What do you mean you saw me with Margie? He frowned."

"Down by the creek, crooning sweet words to her, holding her hand," she replied uneasily.

His brows drew together in a frown, "When was this?"

She felt her cheeks grow warm, "Five years ago, we were to meet at the creek to spend the evening fishing."

Collin's laughter rang out, silencing the crickets and peepers that were singing out.

Viola stomped her foot; her voice shook with fury; "Why you no good shiftless man! I tell you, and all you can do is stand there and laugh at me." Turning on her heel, she stomped off in the direction of the house.

The winds picked up as grass danced candidly about, the sun saying its temporary goodbye as it rested behind the mountains as if it too was done with the conversation.

"Viola, please wait," Collin's feet took to the urgency of catching up with her. Closing the distance between them, he grabbed her wrist, turning her to him. A jolt of lightning ran through his fingers at the mere touch of her.

Her eyes misted with tears as she gazed up into his face. Collin felt the shame of laughing at her to the end of his toes. He had not meant to hurt her feelings; five years was a long time to hold a grudge. Why would she be mad about a boy having his first crush?

"Viola," he gently took her chin in his hand, "I'm sorry, I didn't mean to make you upset. I just thought it was funny that you were mad at me for something that happened so long ago. I do not understand why that would have you upset with me in the first place," his voice soft with emotion.

"It doesn't matter; I'm just foolish anyway." she quietly replied.

"It matters to me, please," he begged, "tell me."

Viola yanked her hand away from his hold, "If you're too simple-minded to figure it out, then forget this whole conversation, don't worry; I can see myself into the house without your help," she hissed.

The darkness of the evening enveloped him in a dreary hug as he untied Maverick; slipping into the saddle, he rode home with a heavyweight hanging over him.

Viola slammed the front door as she raced up the stairs to her bedroom. Throwing herself onto her bed, she let the tears fall; it hurt that he had laughed at her, but most of all, he did not see that it was because she had feelings for him then, and they had only grown stronger since she had been back.

Wiping her eyes, she looked up at the ceiling and cried, God, help heal my heart; my feelings are growing stronger. Please show me what to do, lead me. Amen, Viola silently prayed.

A rooster crowed, awakening the day with smells of fresh air and sunshine. Dragging herself from the soft, warm bed, Viola noticed she had slept later than usual. Quickly performing her morning ablutions, she dressed and braided her hair. Hurrying down the stairs, Viola poured herself a cup of coffee, grabbed a biscuit, and was out the door.

The week was busy with more picking and canning. Viola had not seen or heard from Collin since their walk on Sunday. Her mind was drumming up the conversation that left her with an empty feeling.

She may have been too harsh on him; after all, it was five years ago, and a mind could forget, mostly if it were not something that did not mean anything. Riding into town may give her the respite she needed from overthinking things and canning.

The day brought warmer temperatures as the trees had finished their display of budding new life. The birds circled in the air with their melodic song bound for listening ears as horses and people went about their way. Viola brought the buggy to a halt in front of the mercantile; gathering her skirt, she climbed down from the wagon; circling back to the bed, she looked over jars filled with a lush red sticky goodness. The pots were exquisite, the tops covered with a gingham fabric of vivid red and white that had a coal-black ribbon tied around the lid to give it a fancy look. The mercantile looked forward to when grandmother brought them in to sell. Viola did not tell grandmother when she left, but she brought along extra for Rosebud's Cafe.

Viola's skirts swished as she made her way inside the bright mercantile with everything anyone in this town could need. If the mercantile did not have it, Mr. Tyree could order it from a catalog now that the train ran on the outskirts of town. Mrs. Tyree heard the bell ding about the door; stepping out from behind the counter, she greeted Viola with a hearty hug. "So good to see your back. I'm sure your grandmother couldn't be happier. What brings you in on this fine day," Mrs. Tyree sang.

Clasping her hands behind her back with a giddy smile, Viola rocked back on her heels. "I brought jars of strawberry jam," her eyes sparkling with excitement.

"Oh, I'm so thankful! Customers have been asking about your grandmother's delicious jam. I do not know what is in that dirt, but those strawberries sure do grow better than anyone else's around these here parts. I will have Mr. Tyree unload them from the wagon; then, I can start figuring how much we owe you.

Viola's hand shot out to stop Mrs. Tyree before she hurried off. "Can you have him only take about half of what's in the wagon? I want to see if Rosebud's would be interested in buying the rest."

"Why that is a splendid idea; I'm sure Rosie will be delighted. Can you give me a couple of hours to get the jars unloaded and figure what we owe you?"

Viola clapped her hands together as her eyes twinkled; she would have extra time to have tea at Rosebud's.

"Yes, take your time, I am off to Rosebud's with my jars of jam, and I think I'll have me a mite of tea while I'm there.

The bell over the mercantile door dinged, both ladies turned to see Abby Becker enter. Red curls hung all around her head, a bridge of freckles graced the bridge over her nose, an infectious smile brightened her whole face.

"Viola Branson, I do declare! I heard you were in town; it's so good to see you." Grabbing Viola into a fierce hug, she squealed as they parted.

"You have no idea how much I've missed you! We have so much catching up to do."

Viola squeezed Abby back with an equally tight hug. "It has been quite a while. I am headed over to Rosebud's for tea. Would you care to join me?"

"How delightful, yes, that would be wonderful!" she exclaimed.

Handing her list to Mrs. Tyree, Abby folded her arm through Viola's as they made their way out the door and down the boardwalk to Rosebud's. Viola would have to see if she could drop the jars of jelly off before she left for home. She knew they would be a hit with the customers.

Chapter 7

Horses and buggies littered the street kicking up dust, the train's shrill whistle pulsating in the distance. Everywhere Collin looked, people were going about their business of the day. The week was a prosperous one, with several calves being born, adding to his already increasing herd. He thought about buying himself lunch at Rosebud's to celebrate. He would go over to the livery to see if Boone needed a break, ask him to join him for lunch.

Maverick took on a slow gait; Collin led him to the livery to get some oats and water before going into the livery's front. Boone never minded; after all, Maverick sired from a pure breed stallion that Boone's ~~family~~ family-owned.

The smell of horse and manure assaulted Collin's senses as he strode into the livery. Boone looked up from the horse he was brushing. Wiping the sweat and dirt on his already stained apron; he greeted Collin with a smile.

"What are you doing in town, wrangler?"

Leaning up against the side counter, Collin shrugged his shoulders, "had me a good week, thought I'd come in town for lunch and maybe a conversation with an ugly cowboy like you."

Boone gave a hearty laugh as he smacked Collin on the shoulder. "Is that right? I may have some time to spare, especially if you're paying."

"Oh, I'm paying, but that doesn't mean you can empty my wallet, old friend," he snickered while giving Boone a playful shove.

Taking off his apron, Boone headed for a barrel of water around the back of the shop. Looking over his shouldered, he yelled, "Let me just clean up a bit first."

Once Boone cleaned up, they headed across the street to Rosebud's. Stepping into the café, aromas of baked rolls and fried chicken mingled with laughter and conversations as patrons visited, eating their noontime meal. Collin's eyes had adjusted to the dimmer light. Scanning a place to sit, he saw two heads bent together and heard the giggling that ensued from the pair.

Heart clenching, Collin's face took on a frown at the sight of Viola. He thought about making a hasty retreat. He could tell Boone that he would rather go to the saloon for a bite. Looking over at

Boone, he noticed he had already stepped around him and snagged them a table.

Wouldn't you know he would pick the table right next to Viola and her friend Abby? Casually walking to the table, Collin tipped his hat at the ladies. Viola's eyes met him, and a longing ran through him he had never felt before. Taking his seat, he wanted nothing more than to punch his friend right in the face for sitting here.

Mind numb; Collin had suddenly lost his appetite.

He felt terrible for laughing at Viola when all she did was tell him what he pleaded for her to do. *Boy am I one stupid cowboy*!

Boone kicked him under that table, "Are you going to order or stare at the wall? Emma is waiting to take your order."

Staring up into Emma's face that suddenly turned red, Collin gave her his order.

"What has gotten into you, your usually better company," Boone frowned.

A mixture of sunshine and strawberries tickled his nose, shuffling and scooting of chairs kept him from answering Boone. A tinkling voice thanked Emma for the meal as swishing skirts made their way out the door.

Collin looked back at Boone, who sat smiling like the cat that ate the canary.

Boone leaned back with fingers laced behind his neck as he chuckled, "Man, do you have it bad."

Collin gave Boone a surprised look and, with a downturned mouth, muttered, "Yeah, and I may have messed it all up."

Devouring lunch with small talk as the two men finished their meal. Collin walked with Boone as he made his way back to the livery.

Dark clouds hid the sun as a peal of thunder in the distance made known its presence. The smell of rain and dust swirled about as the winds picked up enough to have people scurrying about to find a place to wait out the storm.

Boone thanked Collin for lunch with a promise of playing cards some evening. Parting way just as Viola passed by in her buggy, making haste to get home before the storm.

Heavy rain pelted the dry earth as lighting zigzagged its way through the sky. Thunder boomed with what sounded like cannons going off.

Collin knew he was in for it; he needed to find a place to shelter until the storm passed. Trees that lined the road took to bending and waving, darkness magnifying as the storm was about to lose its fury.

Maverick whinnied and sidestepped at a tree that fell across the road. Pulling the reins to control Maverick, Collin took on the sight of a wagon on the other side of the downed tree. Sliding off Maverick, he tied the reins to the fallen timber. Crying pierced the air as a strong wind whipped about, blowing debris into his eyes.

Arm over his eyes, he climbed over the log with a nimble swiftness only to see Viola standing beside the buggy with hands swiftly wiping at tears. The wagon's wheel broken, causing it to lean more to one side; it was in no shape to take its occupant home.

Startled, Viola looked up just as Collin pulled her in his arms, tucking her safely beneath his chin. "We need to find a place to hunker down until this storm passes."

Grabbing Viola's hand, the two pushed through scraggy brush, climbing over shifting rock that dotted the land as the rain battered them. If only they could find an overhang to hide under or a cave.

The rain came down like currents in a raging river. Viola tripped over her wet dress, hanging on to Collin's hand as he was pulling her along.

Straight ahead, boulders sat precariously about, forming what looked to be a small space they could use as shelter.

There was barely room for them both to fit. Viola and Collin They stepped into the tight space, Collin felt Viola's body tense.

Sitting on the hard dirt-packed ground, Collin tugged Viola to him, wrapping his arms around her trying to warm her up.

"Once the storm passes, I'll give you a ride home. I can take your wheel to town; I'll get it fixed and bring it to the ranch."

Viola, looking up into Collins's desirous eyes, felt a fire burn in her belly at the closeness they shared. The energy in the air between them had as much force as the storm raging outside the shelter.

Warmth enveloped a cocoon around their bodies. Collin's breath came in an irregular pattern, heart pounding at the scent of strawberries mixed with rain. Viola leaned her soft curvy body into him, he felt Viola tremble in his arms. Looking down at her pink petal-soft lips; he swallowed the lump rising in his throat. Viola's gaze lingered at his mouth, then looking up, their eyes collided with a desire left unsaid. Collin leaned in, his lips landing on hers with an urgency that could not be stilled. His lips savored, teasing, tasting, satisfying the hunger that drove them on. Viola ran her hands up the back of his neck into his hair knocking off his hat. Claiming him with her soft lips as a moan escaped from her throat, the thundering of the storm outside forgotten.

Collin jerked back; he should not have let this happen.

He was afraid Viola would think he was taking advantage of her; that was far from the truth. He had feelings for this incredible woman.

"Viola," his voice tremored, "I'm sorry, I shouldn't have done that."

Blue eyes fluttered open; her kiss swollen lips sighed with contentment.

Her voice quivered, "I'm not the kind of girl who kisses someone I'm not courting; I've never kissed a man before. We have always been friends and well, never mind. I need to get home, grandmother will be worried." She had a way of babbling when she was embarrassed; Viola could not believe she kissed Collin like that.

The fierce wind calmed; a smattering of raindrops lent to the fresh, clean scent that filled the air.

Sunshine was peeking out behind the clouds as it warmed the space they occupied, shining brightly on their faces.

Sliding hurriedly out of the tight space, Viola ran her fingers through her damp tresses, trying to bring them into submission. Viola's dress, wet and muddy from sitting on the ground, was wrinkled with a rip in the hem, her dress was ruined.

Collin squinted as the bright sun broke from the clouds. The sun's rays were shining on the crystal-like water droplets that littered the foliage around them. The smell of clean earth filling his senses.

Brushing at the mud on his pants, he slammed his cowboy hat on his head while taking long strides to catch up with Viola.

"Viola," grasping her arm lightly, he looked down at her, "you have always meant a lot to me. I do not go around kissing every female I encounter. It is different with you. I've missed you, and we are friends, but you're also a beautiful woman, and I care about you."

The cool breeze stirring the trees fluttered Viola's dress, making her shiver. "Collin, if that is true, why did you kiss Margie but not me? I saw you that day we were to go fishing. I thought I would be the one you would want to kiss."

Taking her chin in his rough hands, he tilted her head up to look at him, "I was just a boy back then. Margie was my first real crush, I didn't have genuine feelings for her. That is what young boys do; believe me, I am paying for it still.

Chapter 8

The birds' song carried on the breeze through the trees, the now vibrant blues coloring the sky. Butterflies chased the flowers that swayed about, creating a painter's paradise of the majestic mountains surrounding the beauty of the landscape around them. Viola's soft fingertips touched her lips as the thought of the shared kiss danced in her mind. She was slowly losing her heart to a very handsome and sweet cowboy.

Collin locked his strong, calloused hands together as Viola placed her foot on top, boosting herself into Maverick's saddle. A robust and confident smile stretched across his lips as he mounted, wrapping his muscular arms around Viola and taking the reins. Her body went rigid but then she felt herself relax and give in to the sensation of his broad chest. She leaned back into him with a content sigh. She did not want this moment to end. Collin's soft masculine voice tickled her ear as he whispered to her to look to her left. Two-spotted fawns jumped, playing with each other in the tall grass as they enjoyed their daily exercise.

Viola's eyes big with excitement as she took in their antics giggled with glee, "They are so adorable, where is the mother?" Collin pointed further to the left, just away from the fawns. Momma was eating, watching with cautious eyes as her babies frolicked in the tall grass.

The rest of the ride to the Branson farm was in comfortable silence. Neither wanted to break the magic between them with words but savor the moment.

Viola slid down Maverick with gentle ease; looking up into Collins's face, she shyly asked him to stay for dinner.

"Thank you for the invitation. I need to get back and into some dry clothes. I will hook the wagon up and go back for your broken wheel. I would like to get it into town before Boone leaves for the day. Can I take you up on it when I drop your wheel back off tomorrow?"

A flirty smile crossed her face as she tipped her head back, hand on hip. She batted her long eyelashes, "Only if you promise to take a walk with me after supper."

Collin threw his head back as a throaty laugh pierced the air. "Who is being a flirt now?" he winked with a tip of his hat, riding off as her would-be hero.

Viola was up with the crack of dawn, throwing herself into her work. Trying to keep her mind from wandering back to the kiss with Collin was proving futile. A new day brought with its old fears and doubts that clung to her like a sticktight. What if he just took advantage of the situation? Maybe the kiss meant nothing. The thought of him and Margie laughing about how naive she is, never kissing a man before, made her stomach turn sour. I am not going to think about it; I have laundry to finish.

The slam of the front door snapped her back to what she was doing. The sound of steady footsteps, and flutter of skirts, brought her attention to her grandmother. Grandmother stood over her with a glass of lemonade.

"Thought you could use a glass," her grandmother said as she offered the drink to her.

"That is much appreciated," she drank greedily before handing the cup back.

"Is there something eating at you, child? I've never seen you work so hard flitting about from one thing to another."

"Just a lot on my mind tis all," she hung the sheet on the line with much concentration. With her back to her grandmother, she felt her grandmother's eyes bore into her back.

Grandmother frowned as she picked up a sheet pinning it to the line. "Does this deep thought have anything to do with a certain young man?" she asked, turning to look at Viola's now red cheeks.

Keeping with the chore at hand, Viola looked at grandmother out of the corner of her eye, "How well do you know Collin? Have you ever heard any rumors of him and Margie Vancleet?"

Grandmother's smile slowly spread across her face as she looked into her granddaughter's eyes, "Collin is a fine young man, a hard worker, and helps his neighbors when they need it. When he was a young boy, there was talk he was sweet on Margie, but that was just a passing fancy. That young lady is looking for a husband and will flirt with any eligible cowboy, so don't let her get your dander up."

Face turning red, Viola threw her arms around grandmother, hugging her. "You always keep me centered. What will I do when it's time for me to leave?"

"Maybe I can convince you to stay here. My bones are getting tired, and your help has been a Godsend to me. One of these days, I will have to think about what is best for this ranch and the cowboys who work here. I have been giving thought to leaving it to you. I know if you marry, it will provide you with a dowry of the sort."

Tears slid down Viola's face as she wiped at them, trying to keep her voice steady, "I've been praying about it, since being here. I can't stand to think of leaving you and this beautiful place."

Pulling her granddaughter into a tight hug, she kissed her cheeks, still wet with tears, "Give your cares to the Lord, sweet one, let him guide you. You can never go wrong if you cling tightly to him."

Viola finished putting the roast on a platter when she heard a horse ride up. Peeking out the window, she saw Collin tying Maverick to the hitching post, and long, lean legs carried a confident cowboy to the door.

"Well, don't just stand there; let the man in." grandmother laughed.

Removing her apron, she reached up and patted her hair into place as the golden locks hung down her back, sides pulled up and tucked into place by silver combs.

Viola swung the door open just as the handsome cowboy was about to knock.

Slender fingers reached up to snatch the cowboy hat from his head as an all too familiar smile stretched across his tan face. "Viola, you look beautiful this evening."

"Thank you, won't you come in?" butterflies took flight in a churning nervous stomach as she took a step back and, with a dainty hand, motioned him in.

As Collin stepped past her, she could smell the familiar scent of him. The ~~woodsy scent of the outdoors~~outdoors' woodsy scent mixed with horse and sandalwood enveloped her in toxic headiness that left her weak in the knees. Viola sent up a silent prayer asking God not to let her make a fool of herself this evening.

Viola began putting food on the table as everyone was seated. Heads bowed, and grace said, Collin went to filling his plate. Grandmother passed the roast to Collin with a satisfied smile, "Viola, everything looks and smells delicious."

Chocolate eyes filled with admiration looked up at Viola, "It tastes just as good too; you are an excellent cook."

Red blossomed on her cheeks as she wiped her sweet rosebud lips with her napkin, "Thank you both."

All conversation turned to what was happening in town as the meal began filling their stomach, a summer picnic. Excitement over the activities that would take place was apparent in their voices.

"I heard that there is to be a pie-eating contest, a three-legged race, and Seth Hartag's band will play, not to mention all the food," Viola excitedly sang. The conversation over the picnic ran back and forth among them.

Collin offered to help ~~clearing~~ to clear the dishes from the table. Grandmother felt tired and took up her mending in the parlor leaving the two tasked with putting the kitchen to rights.

Standing with his hip against the sink and towel in hand, Collin tilted his head, "What do you like most about the picnics?"

The warm, sudsy water bringing about a relaxing calm over Viola's hands gave her confidence as she scrubbed the dish in her hand. "I love the dancing; it brings so much cheer. What about you?"

"I have to say the food, but this year I may change my mind."

Her face wrinkled in confusion, "What do you mean?"

Winking with a sly smirk on his lips, he replied, "Holding you for a couple of turns around the dance floor might change my mind to dancing."

Viola's face turned a crimson red as she gave him a shy smile and went back to scrubbing dishes.

With the last dish put away, Viola spoke in a quiet trembling voice, "Would you care to take a walk or sit on the front porch swing?"

The kitchen's stuffiness with all its fantastic smells circulated throughout the room, causing an urgent need for clean, fresh air. Collin's heart pounded, wiping his clammy hands down the front of his jeans, feeling the stiff fabric caress his hands as he mumbled, "A walk would be nice."

The warm evening air hung with the heat of the day as the animals lazed about the barn. The only sounds were that of the water rushing down the mountain pursuing the crystal blue stream below. As Viola and Collin walked, the light wing beauty of butterflies flittered around them, keeping in rhythm with the rest of God's creation while a brown furry bunny finished his evening meal as it dashed across their path.

Viola was falling hard for this rugged cowboy. Her mind told her to run. Her heart wanted him to take her into his arms and kiss her again.

"Viola, would you go to the picnic with me? Collin stared into her eyes as he took her hand. It would mean a lot to me. I could pick you and Grandmother B up int the wagon, she could be our chaperon." Digging into the dirt with the toe of his boot, he held his breath for her answer.

Looking out over the landscape, Viola was speechless, oh, how she wanted to go with him, yet she would be putting her heart in danger. Looking up into those pleading eyes about did her in, "Yes, I would love that," hang her heart, she would deal with it later, right now she just wanted to spend more time with him.

A broad toothy smile took over Collins's face as a fire started in his fingertips traveling to his toes. Keeping Viola's soft petite hand in his, he started walking again.

"Well, now that we have that settled, we can talk about how we are going to win the three-legged race."

Breaking the air's tension with the out-of-the-way question, Viola threw her head back with a throaty laugh as the swishing of her skirts competed with the singing peepers and lowing of the cattle off in the distance.

Chapter 9

The week proved to be a busy one with a few new calves born. Collin and Billy spent long days and most evenings taking care of cattle and fixing things around the farm.

Collin's mind often drifted back to Viola and their walk. She is beautiful, ~~smart~~intelligent, and conversation ~~always~~ continuously flowed smoothly with her. He was getting to know the adult version, and he liked her a lot. Collin could see himself spending his evenings with her in the parlor as she knitted, and he read the paper. Working the ranch and raising children is what his heart had been summoning lately. He knew there was no one else he could see himself doing that with other than Viola.

A bellowing sounded close by, causing him to stop his daydreaming. Tails slapping at the flies as the cows ate on the green grass, calves chased and frolicked about as mommas kept a wary eye on them. The air around him smelled of manure and sweat, and it had Collin looking about his ranch with pride.

Slapping a cowboy hat onto his head, Billy rode up beside Collin. A red scarf tied around his neck with chaps and a black shirt smelling of hard work and the outdoors. Billy pulled Collins's attention away from his daydreaming with his arrival.

"Well, it looks like we finally got everything caught up, boss." Billy ran his hands down his horse's neck, patting and rubbing the smooth skin.

"You sure have been a big help to me this summer Billy, don't know I could have gotten much done without you. Let's head in, get cleaned up, and grab a bite to eat."

People were wandering about hanging welcome signs as children darted about kicking dust-up playing tag as their loud voices mixed with all the excitement. Collin wiped the sweat from his brow as he helped Boone and some of the other men build the stage the band would perform on.

Clearing his throat, Boone looked at Collin with a long quizzical stare. Collin sat back on the heel of his feet. "Why are you looking at me like that?" he grinned.

"Just wondering if you are a coward or if you asked that pretty Viola Branson to the picnic," He bluntly stated.

Collin's expression took on surprise as he laid his hammer down and stared back at Boone's grinning face. "Not that it is any of your business, but I asked her."

"Is she going?" Now it was Boone's turn to be surprised.

Standing to his full height, Collin strode to the water bucket, taking a long draw from the ladle as it satisfied his dry, parched throat. "Why wouldn't she say yes?" an amused smile passing from his mouth. Pouring the water over his sweating head, wiping at his face with his neckerchief, he punched Boone in the arm with a confident laugh.

Boone shook his head, sending sweat flying in Collin's direction; "You are arrogant, you know that?" he guffawed.

Collin let out a hardy laugh, "What about you, cowboy? Did you ask anyone? Maybe Margie Vancleet?"

Boone turned severe eyes on him, "Why would you ask that?"

"I was joking, don't take it so seriously," he huffed.

Boone's face took on a frustrated look; "I know many town folks think she is a flirt, but I think she is lonely. Her daddy throws money at her to keep her out of his way. Margie doesn't have any friends she can confide in about things. Her mother is always off running meetings, entertaining, or shopping. I believe she wants to settle down, but this small town isn't where she belongs."

"How do you know so much about her?" Collin sent him a questioning look.

"I have spent some time with her; she comes into the livery sometimes to get their buggy for the day. She talks to me as a friend, not like some snobby, flirty female."

Collin did not know what to say; that wasn't the Margie he knew. "We better get back to work before the Mayor sees us lollygagging." He smiled.

The warmth of the day was tolerable; the excitement filling Collin's chest gave way to whistling a tune as he pulled on his new cowboy boots and hat. Today was the day he let Viola know he was serious about her, wanted to court her. He could not wait to pick up her and GGrandmother Branson up for the picnic. Wwalking in with the most beautiful women in Once Over on his arm had him giving thanks to God for his goodness.

Pulling up in front of the Branson home, Collin's hands started sweating as his heart took up a gallop. Cattle were munching on grass in the distance; the sound of a harmonica floated on the breeze; a smell of lye soap and leather mixed, causing him to sneeze. Ranch hands were scurrying about to finish their chores, excitement hanging in the air for the day's festivities.

The front door swung open as grandmother and Viola stepped onto the porch. Collins's gaze fell upon her, and a lump took up residence in his throat. There stood Viola in a navy blue dress with pleasts that accented her ~~small~~ tiny waist and womanly curves. Golden locks pulled up with decorative combs; ringlets hung around her pretty pink cheeks, emphasizing her big blue eyes that sparkled upon seeing him. What felt like a hammer hit him square in the chest; he was falling in love with this beautiful woman.

Climbing down from the buggy, he assisted grandmother and her picnic basket up first; turning to Viola, he froze; she smelled of sunshine and ripe strawberries with just a hint of citrus.

Taking her hand, he leaned in and whispered, "You are going to be the most beautiful woman at the picnic. You look lovely in that dress. Is it new?"

Viola's long lashes fluttered as she looked up into his eyes, redness dotting her face. "Thank you, yes, it is. You clean up pretty well yourself, cowboy," she winked as Collin helped her climb into the buggy. The pleasure of her touch searing into Collin's rough big hands.

The buggy jerked with a start as the horses picked up their rhythm as they took off. The excited tones of voices hung on the breeze as they discussed the games they wanted to participate in, along with all the food to eat.

Couples laughed as children ran about playing tag, long tables piled with food lined the area. Blankets spread about with families as little ones already laid their sleepy forms on the blankets. Collin helped the ladies down, grandmother searching for a place to lay their blanket as she took hold of her basket of food she would contribute to the tables.

"I'm going to put this food on the tables; you can lay our blanket out. You two see what trouble you can find," Grandmother sang out as she hurried to the other woman around the food.

Collin took hold of Viola's arm placing it through his and patted her hand. The proud smile found its way across Collin's face as he escorted Viola to a spot to lay the blanket. Sitting down, she thanked him. A giggle and a clearing of someone's throat had him spinning around nose to nose with Boone and a smiling Abby.

"Care if we join you?" Boone's deep voice boomed.

Viola smiled and patted the blanket, "Have a seat, you two."

Abby looked so pretty with a yellow dress and matching ribbon in her red curly hair. Emerald eyes set off her dress, her big smile like a beacon drawing you to herin. "We wanted to see if you would like to watch some of the games with us."

Viola looked up to Collin, who was laughing at something Boone had said. Smiling, she smoothed her dress at her waist, feeling the soft fabric calm her nerves, "Collin shall we walk over and watch the games with Abby and Boone."

Boone nudged him in the arm; "Let's win this three-legged race; what says you?"

Collin shifting from foot to foot, saw Viola give him a nod with a warm smile. "You coming along to watch us win this race?" Collin winked.

Tilting her head to the side, she gave him a sassy smile, "Only if we can make fun of you when you lose."

Boone slapped his hand on his leg, pushing Collin forward as his boisterous laugh rang out.

Stumbling from the push Boone gave him, Collin stretched his hand out to help Viola up. "Let's do this!"

Abby wrapped her arm around Viola's as they trailed after the cowboys; in a low voice, Abby leaned in, "You are smitten with him."

Viola staring straight at Collins's back, only smiled and said, "Can you blame me?" Covering their mouth with their hands, both started laughing. The excitement bouncing around them promised a fun evening at best. Children and adults lined up to enter the race laughing and tying themselves to each other.

Collin and Boone had one of their legs tied together; shoving and goofing around keeping things all in fun.

Old man Jenkins held the gun in the air, "On your mark, get set," bang. The gun-shot told them the race was on.

They took off falling, rolling around on the ground. Boone grabbed Collin's hand, pulling him back up. They took off at an awkward limp but were gaining on the others. Viola doubled over, laughing at the two big men trying to work together, both struggling to lead.

Reaching the finish line, they were about to stumble through when out of nowhere came a ginger striped tabby cat racing by in their path. Collin tried to stop from stepping on its tail by spinning while Boone tried to jump, landing both into each other, knocking heads and falling inches from the finish line.

Viola and Abby squealed with laughter doubled over, wiping tears fighting to gain control of themselves. The crowd cheered and clapped as the cat passed over the finish line. Collin sat with sweat running into his eyes as Boone rubbed his head, each looking a little dazed at what had just taken place. Collin glanced about, spotting Viola; seeing her laughing and wiping her tears made him smile until it was a full force belly laugh at how ridiculous they must look.

The day was turning out to be just about the best day of his life. Stomach full of delicious food, laughing with friends, and best of all, spending time with Viola.

The band started warming up their instruments; Collin was in a toe-tapping mood and couldn't wait to hold Viola in his arms as he spun her around the dance floor. He watched as Viola hugged her grandmother and exchange words. Grandmother Branson was going home, said her old bones had enough for one day. Older folks left, leaving the dancing and courtship up to the younger people.

The evening air started cooling down as it gently nudged the women to wrap shawls around their shoulders; the mixed hues of pink, orange, and blue painted themselves across the sky as if framing the beautiful mountain tops for the perfect romantic evening. An ear-splitting laugh broke through the air breaking up the rhythmic chatter amongst them. Collin knew that laugh, and according to the look on Viola's, so did she.

Collin grimaced as Boone waved to Margie. Abby and Boone had only met up at the picnic as friends since neither had a significant other. Even if Boone was not saying, Collin thought he was sweet on Margie Vancleet.

Margie sauntered over with a smirk on her face; black ringlets hung down her back; she wore a soft rose-colored dress with pleats around the waist that drew the eye. Crystal blue eyes danced as she batted her long eyelashes.

"Well, fancy seeing you all here," fanning the heat from her face with waves of her hand. The band's music struck up a melody as couples took to the platform. Collin wasted no time; he grabbed hold of Viola's hand and guided her to the dance floor.

Stepping into his arms, Viola felt her knees go weak; his masculine smell did funny things to her head; she needed to concentrate, so she did not step on his toes. He twirled her around the dance floor, keeping time with the music. Viola's throat parched from the nearness of Collin's muscular chest and arms that were in direct contact with her. No doubt about it, somewhere she lost her heart to this handsome man.

The music picked up and turned into a quadrille; couples flocked to the dance floor, laughing as they started forming a square. Collin pulled Viola close, "Do you mind if we sit this one out? I'm a little thirsty and could use a cup of punch."

Viola didn't want Collin to let go of her, and they stood there amongst the dancing couples, Collin still holding her in his arms as if he was thinking the same thing. She leaned into his ear and practically shouted, "I could use something to drink as well!" Holding his hand, they stepped from the platform, floating back to the others that were deep in conversation.

Viola sat down on a robust wooden bench that sat off to the sides of the dance floor. "I'll get us a glass of punch," Collin gazed into her upturned face that was all aglow. A smile spread across his face; he lifted her dainty fingers to his warm, soft lips, plating a feather-like kiss to them.

Viola thought she would swoon as he marched off toward the refreshment table to retrieve their punch. Eyes twinkling, taking on a dreamy look, she ran her slender fingers over where his lips had taken residence. She would never forget this night.

Collin approached the refreshment table, forgetting what he was doing as his mind was stuck on holding Viola's soft, warm body in his arms. The sweet scent of strawberries and sunshine teased his nose and mind. Her long silky hair was brushing up against his hand as he pulled her in…

A throat clearing snapped him from his thoughts; there stood Margie, hand on hip with a flirtatious smile on her mouth. "My, one gets mighty thirsty quick from all that dancing,' she tilted her head up and batted her eyelashes. You deserve a good scolding for not dancing with me yet, cowboy," her smile turning to a pout.

Collin reached for the punch glasses ignoring Margie. Turning to push past her, a strong, firm hand shot out, grabbing his arm. Trying not to spill the drinks, Collin steadied his arm; looking up into eyes that took on a determined glint, Margie swung him around, stepping between his arms and planting a kiss right on his lips.

A giggle escaped her lips as she licked them, enjoying the shocked look on Collin's face at the same time he heard a loud gasp. There stood Viola, her confused face twisted in anger and hurt as her eyes took on a misty display, hands pressed to her mouth as she let out a choked cry.

Collin froze, watching as if it were playing out between another couple; his feet would not cooperate with his head, he could not move.

Viola turned, holding her skirts as she ran into the crowd.

Collin turned toward Margie, anger flashing across his face as he felt red creeping up his neck. Dropping the cups, he barked out, "I am sick of your ridiculous flirting; I have tried to be nice about it, but not anymore. Please leave me alone, do not ever talk to me again. I am not interested in you and never will be." Muttering under his breath as he stomped away, "Now I have to try and fix the mess you made." Collin didn't even care that he had left a crying Margie standing with a crowd of onlookers.

Pushing through the people, Collin looked everywhere for Viola. Wiping hands down his sad face, he thought he might start crying himself. Why did Margie always have to have every man's attention? Things were going so well between him and Viola, and now this. She would never trust him with her heart again; he was sure.

Viola could not see where she was going as the tears came fast and hard, causing her body to tremble. A gentle female's voice called after her begging her to wait, to stop running. Collapsing in the tall grass as the sobs racked her body, soft arms drew her into an embrace. Abby was rocking her back and forth as she let Viola cry.

Once the tears remained at only a trickle, and deep shuttering breaths came, Abby pulled Viola at arm's lengths. "Honey, it will be okay. Men are so addle-brained; I don't think he likes Margie as much as he does you. I see the way he looks at you. You should go talk to him."

Viola sat up straight, "Absolutely not. If he wants that tarte, he can have her, they deserve each other! Can you give me a ride home? I don't want to stay anymore, and I do not want him giving me a ride home."

Abby pulled her in for a tight hug, "If that's what you want, I will get my parents, and we will leave."

Sun streamed in the window, awaking Viola; squinting, she covered her eyes with her arm. A headache the size of Texas was pounding in her temples. Eyes red and puffy blinked as memories from last night's fiasco came clamoring back to her. A moan escaped her throat as she rolled over, pulling the covers up over her head. Staying in bed was what she would do today; she would tell Grandmother she didn't feel well.

Grandmother opened Viola's door as stuffiness from the sun-filled room rushed to meet her. There under the covers lay Viola, still sound asleep. Grandmother's quiet footsteps shuffled into the room; she moved to open the window, pushing the curtains back, letting in a cool breeze stirring a sleeping Viola.

"Someone sure is sleeping late this morning, GGrandmother rested her hand on Viola's forehead. Are you feeling sick, dear?"

The cool breeze flitted across Viola's face as the smell of fresh air filled her nostrils. Her headache was fading, but her heart was still hurting. "I'm not feeling so good this morning, Grandmother. I think it must have been something I ate," the lie slipped from her tongue, turning to regret. She never lied to her grandmother before. The pain was too much to share right now; all she wanted to do was fall back to sleep and forget.

"Well, why don't you rest? I will bring you some water and a bit of broth." Grandmother patted her hand to reassure her that she would have her better in no time.

Viola woke with a start; the dark of the night filled her room as the cold air of the mountain blew her curtains around. Shivering, she pulled her shawl from off the bed, throwing it around her shoulders as she stumbled to close the window. Her headache was gone, but a lone tear slipped down her cheek. How would she go on without Collin? She had fallen in love with him at some point during her time here. Her heart for the mountains and her grandmother begged her to put down roots and stay but seeing Collin would be too painful. She knew she had to leave. The strawberries were all canned and put away; Grandmother could handle everything else. Telling Grandmother that she was going back to St Joseph, Missouri, would be so hard.

Softly slipping downstairs with the bible in hand, Viola lit a lamp on the kitchen table. She would drink some tea and read her bible; it always held the answers to comfort her.

With a teacup filled with hot tea, she turned her bible to chapter twenty-nine, verse eleven in Jeremiah. "For I know the plans I have for you, declares the Lord, 'plans to give you hope and a future." Maybe this was God's way of telling her she needed to go back home that Collin wasn't the one for her. She would talk with Grandmother first thing in the morning about returning home.

Viola found grandmother sitting at the kitchen table the next morning, drinking a cup of coffee. Filling a cup with coffee for herself, she sat across from Grandmother.

"Are you feeling better this morning?" Grandmother blew on the swirling black liquid, trying to cool it some.

Viola looked down at her fingers splayed around her cup, "A little, but there is more to it than what I told you yesterday."

A look of surprise flickered across grandmother's face. "What do you mean?"

"I've decided to go back home." Viola's eyes were feeling with tears as she sniffed them back.

Letting out a sigh, "I don't understand; I thought you were leaning toward staying here. What happened?"

Tears fell down her face as Viola lifted her cup to her lips with shaking hands. "Collin is interested in Margie, and I can't stay around here and watch him court her."

Grandmother reached across the table, taking Viola's hand in her own, rubbing her thumb across the top. "I find that hard to believe; I see how that boy looks at you. He has been sniffing around here since you showed up. What makes you think that is true?"

Viola looked up at grandmother with tear-stained cheeks, "We were having a great time until he went to get us some punch. I went looking for him because he had been gone for a while; I saw him and Margie kiss.

Grandmother took a deep breath, "What did you do?"

"I ran. I didn't want Collinthem to see me crying. I felt like snatching Margie's hair out of her head and dumping the punch on his head, but I knew that wouldn't be a wise example of God's love, so I ran. I had Abby, and her parents bring me home."

Grandmother walked around to Viola and hugged her to her side, "Promise me you will pray about this. I think it would be wise to talk with Collin before you make any rash decisions."

Viola wrapped her arms around her grandmother, "I have thought on this, all night. I have to leave at the end of the week."

The week flew by, with Viola and Grandmother spending time fishing and reminiscing about the days when her mother was a young girl. Viola's heart broke. She didn't want to leave the family, friends, and the land she loved.

Viola decided to ride out to the Becker farm to tell Abby she was leaving early in the morning.

Cows grazing on the lush green grass bawling with pleasure from their meal stared as Viola drove by in the wagon. The hot day drew down on her with heaviness. The large log house set back up against a small forest with a large porch currently housing an old dog named Ben. The farm was quaint and showed the love of hard work with its flower beds and long straight rows of the abundant garden.

Viola set the brake, shielding her eyes to get a better look around against the sun's rays; she spotted Abby. A smile spread across her lips that ended up in a slight giggle. There stoodwas Abby dressed in trousers, an old worn shirt with a battered old hat perched on her head that held the long braid that ran down her back.

Abby loved growing her sunflowers and took her job seriously. Viola could see Abby bent over, touching plants, checking the soil, and talking to them in a sweet mother voice.

Viola climbed down from the wagon; with bonnet strings waving and her boots drowning in the soft grass, she made her way to Abby.

"Looks like your sunflowers are doing well!" Viola smiled.

Hand thrown over heart Abby gave a jump; "You bout scared me plumb to death." she gasped.

Viola snickered as she stepped up, giving her a gentle hug. "Will you take a break? I came to tell you something important."

Abby's shot her a concerned look, "Yes, let's get a glass of cool water and sit on the porch."

Walking with an easy cantor to the porch, the two talked about the sunflowers. Viola gently sat in the rocking chair as Abby poured a tall glass of water.

Flopping into the other chair Abby took a long drink, resting her eyes on Viola; "Tell me what is going on."

Hands folded into a fist, Viola's words rushed out, "I am leaving tomorrow morning."

Abby choking on her water, spat out, "Why?"

"I cannot live here and watch Collin and Margie together, so I am going back to St Joseph. Grandmother went to town and purchased my ticket."

"Viola, why don't you go talk to him about all of this, don't make any hasty decisions until you do."

Viola shook her head; "No, this is the second time he has broken my heart. I just wanted to say goodbye. I will miss you, Abby."

Morning gave way to silent tears running down Viola's face. The hand-stitched quilt with all its vibrant colors made her feel safe and warm. The smell of vanilla touched everything in the room, giving the warm scent of grandmother's presence. Folding her belongings, she carefully placed them in the trunk, ready to depart for the train station. Looking up at the ceiling, Viola sent a silent plea to God to give her the strength to do this.

Jude carried her trunks out to the wagon as she hugged grandmother.

"Child, are you sure this is what you want?" Grandmother cupped the side of Viola's face.

"Yes, grandmother," Viola bent down and placed a gentle kiss on her grandmother's cheek.

Lifting a basket to place in her granddaughter's hand, Grandmother wiped a lone tear from her face. "God, go with you and do not forget to write."

Jude helped Viola into the wagon; she turned and waved as the wagon rolled on.

Chapter 10

Collin was working himself into an early grave, trying to forget about Viola. Flies buzzing around the hot barn as the smell of fresh manure waft around the stalls, Maverick whinnied as his tail swatted at the flies. Collin threw another bale of hay to Billy.

"Boss, can we stop for a drink of water? I am hot and tired, you have worked us to the bone this week." Billy's exhausted look stopped Collin from lifting the next bale.

"Sorry Billy, yes, we can stop for a rest. I have a lot on my mind, is all."

Billy took his hat off, swiping the back of his hand across his forehead. "Does it have anything to do with Miss Branson?"

Collin's eyes snapping to Billy, "What makes you think that?"

"Well, because of what happened at the picnic. The whole town is talking about it, and you haven't seen Viola all week."

"Everybody needs to mind their own business, that's what!" Collin stomped off toward the house.

Collin was exhausted but another day without seeing and holding Viola in his arms made him want to crawl back in bed and sleep. The smell of bacon he stood frying filled the air as his stocking feet padded across the kitchen floor to get a plate. Steam coming off the coffee as Collin he blew on it to cool it some. He had become a shell of a man without Viola beside him. Collin longed to take her in his arms and press his lips to her sweet tasting ones.

A banging on the door drew him from his depressed state. Collin wondered who would be at his door so early in the morning; it wasn't even fully light out.

Striding across the worn kitchen floor, Collin opened the door to Abby Becker, who paced back and forth, wringing her hands.

With a surprising catch in his voice, "Abby, what are you doing here?"

Abby grabbed hold of his shirt and gave him a firm shake. "What are you doing still here?" She screeched.

Collin took hold of her tiny but strong hand and removed it from his shirt as he took a step back. "I live here, that is what I'm doing here."

Abby's eyes grew big, "Why aren't you at the train station?"

Collin gave her a puzzled look, "Why would I be at the train station?"

"I thought you knew; we have to hurry!" she shouted.

"Please calm down; you are not making any sense." Collin took hold of her shoulders, looking her in the eyes.

"It's Viola; she is leaving on the train this morning to go back to Missouri. Collin, she is in love with you, she said she couldn't live here watching you with Margie."

Collin slid his large, calloused hands down his face. Why had he been so stubborn? Collin~~He~~ should have talked to Viola and told her what happened. He was mad at her for ~~she~~ even thinking~~ought~~ he had a thing for Margie. Collin~~He~~ was waiting for her to apologize for doubting him. What was he thinking? Now she was leaving for good. Collin could not breathe suddenly as if his breath were going on the train with Viola. He had to stop her; she was his world, and he had to convince her of that.

Grabbing his hat from the peg by the door, he took off at a run, "Abby, what are you waiting on? Let's go stop her," he hollered over his shoulder.

The horses were kicking up dust as Collin urged them on faster; landscape rushed past as the wind whipped his hat about, trying to wrestle it from his head. Abby clung to the side of the wagon, knuckles white from her firm hold.

Steam rose off the engine as it pulled into the station with a loud whistle. People were rushing off the train, searching for loved ones stirring up air and dust that settled.

Viola took hold of her reticule; she was ready to board and would save the crying until later.

Collin spotted her first. Jumping down from the wagon with horses lathered up from being driven so hard ~~he forgot all~~, he forgot about helping Abby down. Running onto the platform with boots clomping, he ran into Viola as she stood up, almost knocking her over.

Viola looked up with startled eyes as rough hands grabbed her by the shoulder to keep her from falling over. There stood Collin face to face with her. A shudder racked her body as her eyes filled with tears. Collin didn't ask for permission; he pulled her into his arms and kissed her softly at first but then with a hunger that told what words could not.

Viola pulled back as tears slid down her face, wiping at them with her gloved hands. She looked up at Collin with so much love in her eyes that he wanted to kick himself for not coming to her sooner.

"Why are you here?" She stuttered.

"Viola, I'm so sorry. I should have come to talk to you sooner, but my stupid pride got in the way. I know what you think you saw that night at the picnic, but it's not what you think. I had my hands full with our drinks, and Margie would not leave after I all but ignored her. The next thing I know, she stepped between my arms and kissed me. I froze; I was shocked that she would do that. When you ran off, I'm afraid I was rather mean to her in front of everyone. Viola, you are the only one I want. I love you, and I have since I laid eyes on you the day your grandmother invited me to have lunch with you at Rosebuds. Please, do not leave. Stay here with me where you belong."

Viola stood as rigid as a tree; her heart and mind were fighting a battle within her. She loved Collin, but could she trust him?

"Viola," Collin's voice wrapped around her heart and squeezed. He cupped the side of her face rubbing his finger over her jaw. "Please, I know you love me too, or at least I think you do. I never gave Margie a single reason to think I wanted anything to do with her. She needs a friend, someone like you that can lead her to God and his love. She is looking in all the wrong places because she is lonely. I know this because of what Boone told me about her."

Viola stood on tiptoes and pulled Collin's head to her so she could claim his lips. "I love you too, Collin." She spoke with a gentleness that pierced his heart.

Collin slipped down to one knee taking her hand in his; "Marry me? I want to grow old with you, have lots of children and sit on the front porch in our rockers. We can tell our grandchildren about the summer you came home to help your grandmother with strawberries, only to fall in love with a stubborn old cowboy."

"Yes, oh yes!" Viola squealed. Collin grabbed her, turning her in circles, laughing as pure love flitted across her beautiful face.

Collin grabbed her hand and led her back to the wagon and into his life where she belonged.

Epilogue

Viola sat on the front porch with the warmth of the day, a black and white puppy curled up at her feet. The blue sky against the backdrop of the mountains promised a beautiful day. Collin handed her a cool drink that she took and pressed up to her forehead. "You seem a million miles away." Collin smiled, taking a sip of his refreshment.

"Just thinking how blessed I am, rubbing her stomach at the little kick that had only started days ago, Viola turned her sparkling eyes to Collin. Grandmother giving us her ranch and living with us to help with this little one once its time means so much. I never thought that strawberry summer would turn into all of this; she swept her hand through the air, landing on her belly.

Collin gazed out over the green land with pastures bursting with cattle. The quiet all around them except for the few birds that sang out their praise; he let out a sigh as he rocked back in his chair. "God certainly has been good to us. He had a plan all along for our lives, Mrs. McKenny.

Standing up, Collin took her hands and helped her from her chair. Pulling her into his arms, he kissed the end of her pert little nose.

Viola stood on tiptoes as she planted a soft kiss on his lips, "I love you, Mr. McKenny, for now and for always, but you are still not getting out of picking strawberries."

The End

About the Author

Shonda Czeschin Fischer is a wife and mother of 2 who has been married for 21 years to her husband Craig. She has worked alongside her husband in children's ministry for 17 years. Shonda loves reading, reviewing books and anything that has to do with history. She lives in Missouri where she spends time with her shih tzu Daisy and her Siamese cat Nala. Shonda loves to talk about God and enjoys encouraging and lifting others up.

If you enjoyed reading this story, please consider leaving a review on Amazon or Goodreads.

You can visit my Facebook page at Author Shonda Czeschin Fischer or email me at Shondaczeschinfischerauthor@gmail.com.

I love hearing from my readers and will try to respond promptly.

Coming soon!

Snowflower Fall

Once Over Series, Book 2

Made in the USA
Monee, IL
22 April 2021